For Gurbani, my sunflower.
—MSG

First published in the United States in 2022 by Sourcebooks. · Text © 2021, 2022 by Monika Singh Gangotra · Illustrations © 2021, 2022 by Michaela Dias-Hayes · Cover and internal design © 2022 by Sourcebooks · Sourcebooks and the colophon are registered trademarks of Sourcebooks. · All rights reserved. · The characters and events portrayed in this book are fictitious or are used fictitiously. Any similarity to real persons, living or dead, is purely coincidental and not intended by the author. · The illustrations were created using watercolor and fabric scans, with the final art completed digitally. · Published by Sourcebooks Jabberwocky, an imprint of Sourcebooks Kids · P.O. Box 4410, Naperville, Illinois 60567-4410 · (630) 961-3900 · sourcebookskids.com · Originally published in 2021 in the United Kingdom by Owlet Press. · Cataloging-in-Publication Data is on file with the Library of Congress. · Source of Production: 1010 Printing Asia Limited, Kwun Tong, Hong Kong, China · Date of Production: December 2021 · Run Number: 5024414 · Printed and bound in China. · OGP 10 9 8 7 6 5 4 3 2 1

"Why shouldn't I drink too much tea?" asked Amrita.

"It's silly old wives' tales, my darling. For years, people would avoid or eat certain foods, wear smelly creams, or stay out of the sun, thinking it would make their skin lighter. They thought that was more beautiful than having darker skin."

Amrita wrinkled her nose. "That's ridiculous."

"I know, Beta. It's nonsense," Mom sighed and gave Amrita a kiss. "We need to teach them that the skin we are in is EXACTLY as it is meant to be."

The big day arrived. "Look at all these beautiful colors, Amrita."
Mom smiled. "Which one would you like to wear?"

Amrita clapped her hands in delight. "I want to look just like the sunflower in our
garden!" Amrita grinned. "It's so pretty and just as tall as me. So...yellow please!"

SUNFLOWER SISTERS

WORDS BY
MONIKA SINGH GANGOTRA

PICTURES BY
MICHAELA DIAS-HAYES

sourcebooks
jabberwocky

"It's a lovely day for a celebration," said Mr. Jones from next door.

"My sister Jas is getting married!" Amrita squealed while helping Dad hang the lights.

"And my brother Yemi's getting married too." Amrita's friend Kiki grinned.

"It's so bright today," chirped Ms. Laurette. "Would you girls like sunscreen? We don't want your beautiful skin to burn."

"Yes please," the girls said in unison.

"Look! Our guests have arrived," Amrita's dad said. "There's still lots to do."

As Amrita got ready for a cup of masala chai after her bath, Dondi gave her a squeeze.

"Yes you really are beautiful like the leaves in autumn. Do you know people travel from miles around to see the browns and golds of the changing leaves? It's a marvel just like you."

"Don't let Amrita drink too much tea," Aunty said with a grumpy grimace. "And we told you every day when you were pregnant with Amrita to drink saffron and milk, but did you listen…?"

"Oh Aunty, not this nonsense again!" Dad said, rolling his eyes. "Come on, Amrita. Time for bed."

Aunty hugged Amrita with a tight squeeze.
"My, how you've grown! Come in out of the sun—
you don't want to get a tan before the wedding!"
Dad shook his head and sent the girls inside.

"Jas! What is that on your face?" cried Amrita. Mom was not pleased at all.

"Aunty brought this cream over for me, to make my skin look fair and bright for the wedding," said Jas, looking unsure.

"Ewww! What if Shahid doesn't recognize you?" Amrita and Kiki laughed.

"Don't tease your sister, Amrita." Aunty frowned. "You'll miss her when she is married and moved out. Jas needs to look her absolute best for her big day! Besides, maybe you should try…"

"Oh, stop Aunty!" snapped Mom. She took Jas's hand and lovingly wiped the cream off her face. "Your skin is lovely just as it is, my precious daughter. Tomorrow you'll be the most beautiful bride anyone's seen." Mom smiled.

"I have to go home now," Kiki said, giving Amrita a good-bye hug.

"Here, take some treats and be sure to give our blessings to your brother and family, Kiki," said Mom. "We hope you all have a wonderful celebration tomorrow."

Mom turned to Amrita. "It's time for your bath, Beta. Come on, up those stairs."

"Here, let me help Amrita," said Dondi. "We'll have you sparkling as white as snowdrops for the wedding tomorrow."

"EEK! Dondi, stop, that tickles!" Amrita giggled.

"Snow drops?" gasped Mom, creating a whirlpool in the bath water. "No! I prefer golden-brown autumn leaves swirling and whirling in the breeze!"

"YELLOW?!" gasped Aunty, entering the room. "With YOUR complexion?"

"I have just the outfit for you Amrita," whispered Mom. "Follow me. I've been saving it for just the right moment..."

"My mother gave it to me when I was your age," Mom revealed as she handed down the box.

"Mom, why was Aunty surprised when I chose yellow?" Amrita asked.

"Well, some people think that wearing certain colors makes our skin look darker," Mom said.

"But shouldn't we wear colors that make us happy?" Amrita asked. "Our skin is beautiful whatever color we wear, right?"

"That's right, Amrita," Mom said. "When I wore this outfit, my mom said I reminded her of the sun. Warm and kind. And yellow has been my favorite color ever since."

"Do I look like the sun too?" asked Amrita.

"You look even more beautiful, just like the tall sunflowers, proud and radiant," Mom said, beaming.

"Then I will always look up toward you, because you are my sun," Amrita replied, holding Mom's hand tightly.

The wedding was wonderful. Amrita felt amazing in her yellow lehenga.

After the ceremony, as Jas was saying goodbye to her family, Amrita twirled like a sunflower spinning towards the sunshine. She wanted to remember this happy feeling as she closed her eyes, enjoying the warmth on her face.

Aunty watched Amrita dancing. "She looks so beautiful in that outfit," Aunty whispered to Amrita's mom, "and I am sure your mom would have been very happy to see her wearing it today too."

Amrita's mom looked towards the sun with a teary smile.

Just then, Amrita heard something...

Music! Kiki's family was celebrating a wedding on the other side of the street. Amrita's eyes opened wide as she looked a little closer and spotted something.

Another little sunflower with a beautiful face looking up at the sun...

It was Kiki! In a sea of yellow and boldest blue!

Amrita grabbed Mom's hand
and pulled her across the road.

Kiki and her mom let Amrita peek inside to see waves of yellow, gold, and blue twirling around the dance floor. Everyone cheered and sang as Yemi and his bride were showered with money while they danced. This was a day that Amrita and Kiki would never forget.

Outside, their mothers smiled at each other knowingly, as the girls made each other promise. From that moment on, they would make each other feel like sunflowers every day.

"SUNFLOWER SISTERS!"
they both laughed as they locked fingers and then gave each other the biggest hug.

And they never broke their promise...

WHAT IS COLORISM?

Colorism is a system of prejudice or discrimination in which people are treated differently because of the shade, tone, or color of their skin. People may be seen as more beautiful or of a higher class because they have lighter colored skin compared to other people in their own community who have darker skin. This often happens between people of the same race, but this bias can also come from people of another race too. A lot of history has contributed to what much of the world sees as beautiful.

WHY IS THIS BAD?

Unfortunately, some people (including family members) can think this way. This can make darker-skinned people very sad. They might even try to make their skin lighter (sometimes in very dangerous ways) just to try and fit in: using harmful skin-lightening creams, undergoing surgical treatments, and eating or avoiding certain foods. Some people don't even play in the sunshine, thinking it will make their skin darker. It is our job to help them see why this is wrong. The best way to do this is with learning and kindness. The more information you have, the better equipped you are to change things around you.

WHAT CAN WE DO TO CHANGE THIS?

Talk, listen, and learn about colorism. If you want more information, ask a grown-up if they can help. You may be small, but you have a big voice. Speak to your friends, teachers, siblings, and caring adults about colorism. If you see or hear anything that doesn't sound like kindness about another person's skin color, use your brave voice to tell them that all the shades of the skin color rainbow are beautiful.

Love yourself. When you look in the mirror every morning, after brushing your teeth, say to yourself, "I AM DIFFERENT AND THAT MAKES ME BEAUTIFUL!" We think your skin is beautiful and you are awesome just the way you are. And most importantly, be someone's sunflower. Loving one another for who we are is a great way to change the world!